In memory of Nasrin Khosravi,
who brought color into the lives
of children.

Text copyright © 2013 by Uma Krishnaswami
Illustrations copyright © 1999 by Nasrin Khosravi
Illustrations first published in *Dokhtare Baghe Arezoo* in Iran in 1999 by Tooka
Published in Canada and the USA in 2013 by Groundwood Books

The quotation on page 28 is from Hans Christian Andersen: *The Complete
Fairy Tales and Stories*, translated by Erik Christian Haugaard,
Doubleday, 1974, p. 1070.

Groundwood Books / House of Anansi Press
110 Spadina Avenue, Suite 801, Toronto, Ontario M5V 2K4
or c/o Publishers Group West
1700 Fourth Street, Berkeley, CA 94710

We acknowledge for their financial support of our publishing program the
Canada Council for the Arts, the Government of Canada through the Canada
Book Fund (CBF) and the Ontario Arts Council.

 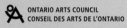

Canada Council   Conseil des Arts
for the Arts   du Canada

ONTARIO ARTS COUNCIL
CONSEIL DES ARTS DE L'ONTARIO

Library and Archives Canada Cataloguing in Publication
Krishnaswami, Uma
The girl of the wish garden : a Thumbelina story / written by
Uma Krishnaswami ; illustrated by Nasrin Khosravi.
Based on Thumbelina by Hans Christian Andersen.
ISBN 978-1-55498-324-7
I. Khosravi, Nasrin II. Andersen, H. C. (Hans Christian),
1805-1875. Tommelise. III. Title.
PZ7.K75Gi 2013   j813'.54   C2012-905126-8

The illustrations were done in acrylic and tissue on paper, the cover on linen.
Design by Michael Solomon
Printed and bound in China

MIX
Paper from
responsible sources
FSC
www.fsc.org   FSC® C018479

THE GIRL OF THE WISH GARDEN

A Thumbelina Story

Uma Krishnaswami

PICTURES BY

Nasrin Khosravi

GROUNDWOOD BOOKS
HOUSE OF ANANSI PRESS
TORONTO   BERKELEY

IN A LAND of dreams, where time itself
can shift and change,
I once saw this tale unfold.

The child was named Lina.
Her mother had found her in a silken flower
in a garden of wishes, where the birds sang wild
and the winds blew free.

"Child of wildness, child of freedom,"
her mother sang to Lina.
"Blessed may you be,
and lucky am I to have found you."

But even while she sang her fondest hopes
for her tiny daughter,
she worried, for many dangers wait upon a girl
no bigger than a thumb.

Indeed, it happened that a giant frog
snatched Lina up
and took her to his water-lily pond,
thinking her to be a bright toy
or perhaps a tasty morsel.

The frog deposited her upon a lily pad
and swam away to look for more such jewels.

"Help me!" Lina shouted,
but her voice was drowned out
by the splash of water
and the juddering of leaf stem.

Held prisoner by the ripples,
she cried great tears.

As Lina's tears ran dry,
an old wild tune crept
into her mind. She sang:
"Wind-swish, bird-flutter,
fish-bubble and all,
come to me now,
come when I call."

In answer, the pond grew thick with curious fish.
Lina showed them how to snip and where to chew,
and soon they cut the leaf free of its stem,
so it floated like a raft.

But oh! It drifted into a thicket of weeds
where crazybugs chattered and swarmed.
"Look, look!"
"A two-legs!"
"How funny it is!"
"No feelers?"
"No pincers?"

"Get away!" cried Lina. "Leave me alone!"
But still the crazybugs clustered and thronged
and chattered endlessly.
"It's a cranky, pushy two-legs!"
"Wild creature!"
"Child of winds!"

Winds! Wildness! A tune came back to Lina
on butterfly wings:
"Wind-swish, bird-flutter,
leaf, sail me free,
lift me away,
as high as a tree."

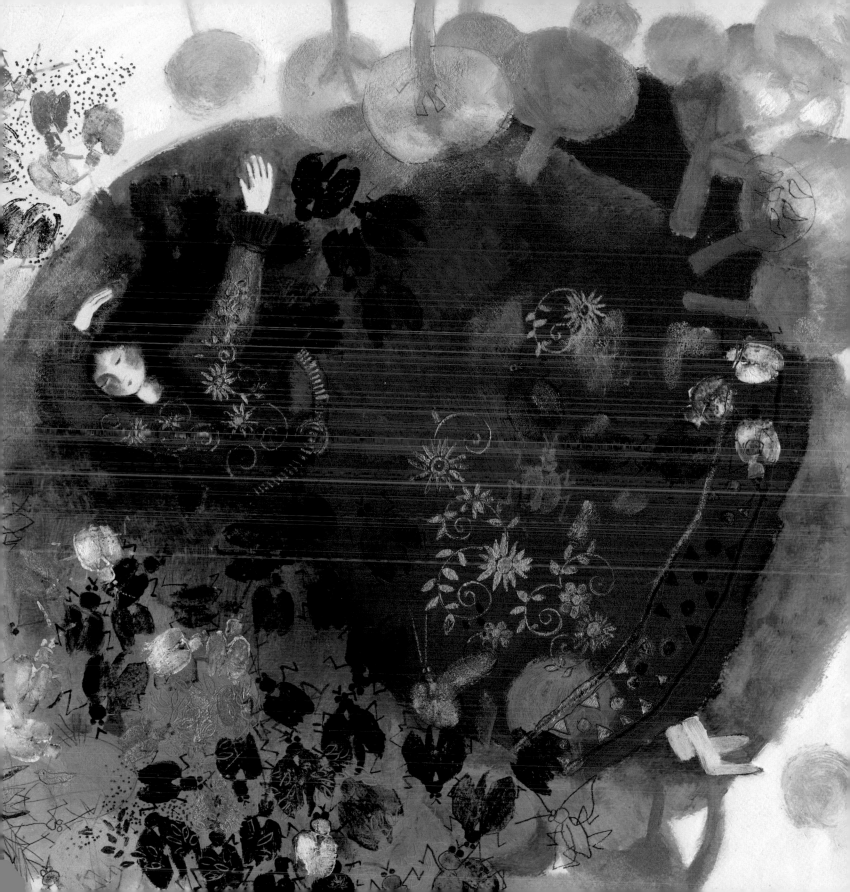

She kicked and paddled with all her might,
until her lily pad pulled free.
It lifted her into the sky and sailed her down,
down into the lap of a tree in the depths of a forest.

All summer, Lina lived in that forest.
She chased small ghost creatures
that skittered through the undergrowth.
She wove a bed of wild grasses
and found nectar and pollen for food
and dewdrops to quench her thirst.

But soon the seasons shifted and the cold closed in upon her,
and she yearned for the warmth of another living soul.

Surely there was someone
who could keep her company and be her friend.
She looked everywhere, until she came upon the door
of a small, half-hidden house. A mouse answered her knock.

"What have we here?" said the mouse.
"A tuckered-out two-foot. Come in, come in.
No need to thank me. Just give me a hand with the chores."

Lina peered into the dimly lit mouse hole and trembled,
for who can read the intentions of mice with sharp teeth
and quivering whiskers?

Then she heard music curling like vines in sunlight,
until it seemed that birds from her dreams
feathered her heart,
so she went in.

The mouse was kind enough to Lina in her own grumpy way.
Lina, in turn, swept and mopped the little mouse house,
which was badly in need of dusting and tidying.

One day in a back room,
Lina tripped over something soft and feathered —
a swallow!

"It's just a dead bird," said the mouse.

"Poor thing," Lina whispered. She took off her coat
and laid it over the sad, cold feathers.

A song welled up inside her:
"Wind-whisper, bird-warble,
bug-swarm now and then,
breathe the bird in, breathe it back.
Make it live again."

"What a racket you're making," said the mouse.

But Lina thought she saw the swallow's wing tremble.

Every day after that,
in between sweeping and mopping,
tidying and dusting, Lina gathered food
for her swallow — seeds of sunflower and millet
and a little cracked corn.

The mouse seemed surprised that she would care a squeak
for a worthless dead bird.

How still the swallow was! It would not eat the grain
nor drink the droplets of water that Lina saved
in a thimble.
Was the mouse right?
Was the bird dead?

A wounded song
came bursting from Lina:
"Wing-tremble, bird-cry,
take my hope and sorrow.
Make my bird breathe again.
Let it fly tomorrow."

The fragile song
folded itself around the bird's still body.
Uneasily, Lina waited and watched.
Was that a breath? She dared not look.

Slowly, surely, the swallow revived,
ate a little grain, drank water from the thimble.

Lina hugged her swallow friend.
"I wish with all my heart," she said,
"that we could go together
away to where the sun shines bright
and the winds blow free
and music makes dreams
come true."

At once, music poured out from all around —
earth-drums from beneath her feet,
chimes of breeze and purl of stream
and harmonies of stars.

"I've been waiting for you," said the swallow.
"Come with me to that land of dreams,
to the garden of wishes where stories are made
by the folding of time."

Lina rode away on the back of her swallow friend,
until they reached a warm land where the sun shone kindly,
casting an image upon the surface of a rippling lake.

"Mother!" cried Lina, and tried to run to her.
But the reflection flickered
like memory, and she ran instead
into the map of her own life
spread out like a carpet —
all of it, birdsong and lonely fear, wind-chime and mouse-fret
and illuminations of what was yet to come.

Wait! Listen! A surge of song,
and the swallow was gone.
Someone held a hand out to Lina,
expecting nothing in return.

In the place of a mouse squeak
was the fine, fierce whinny
of a storm horse.

Spare as thought and clear as wishes are to dreamers,
the two sang together, rode together.
They flew high as glory, long and far,
until they disappeared
from my sight,
leaving only the breath
of the living wind.

In 1836, the Danish poet and storyteller, Hans Christian Andersen, published the original tale of a tiny girl found in a flower. A year later, he wrote:

> …the poet is always poor; honor, therefore, is the golden bird he
> tries to grasp. Time will tell whether I can catch it by telling fairy
> tales.

Andersen called his tiny girl Tommelise. Most English translations change her name to Thumbelina. Author Erik Christian Haugaard, who shared both Andersen's Danish heritage and his middle name, preferred to call her Inchelina. Here she is simply Lina.

I was a child growing up in India when I first encountered the stories of Hans Christian Andersen in a picture book. I was about eight years old. Somewhere between the images and words, I learned that stories could stir me, make me laugh, move me to tears.

Much as I revered them, however, I never felt I could lay cultural claim to Andersen's tales. Then I learned about an unexpected migration of this story. In 1999, a Farsi picture-book version had been published in Iran, featuring the luminous artwork of Nasrin Khosravi. Her pictures, with their delicate lines, glowing palette and mirage-like details, focus on some elements of the story, mute or shift others and completely ignore a few. They spoke to me as Andersen's stories had done.

Sadly, Nasrin Khosravi died before I became acquainted with her work, but creating text for it has been an honor and privilege. I used the pictures as my primary source material, trying to grasp their emotional arc as if it were that elusive golden bird. In general, where the art departed from Andersen's narrative, I followed. At the same time, I did my best to keep certain features of Andersen's immortal wonder tales: the presence of a poet narrator, a read-aloud quality, shifting landscapes, and the pull and tug of storyline.

PUBLISHER'S NOTE

We are pleased to publish this book in memory of Nasrin Khosravi and would like to thank her children, Sam Moshaver and Ava Moshaver, for providing us with the illustrations.

Nasrin Khosravi was a world-renowned illustrator of children's books. Born in Tehran, Iran, she graduated from Tehran University in graphic and fine arts, taught illustration at Honar University and illustrated more than thirty-five books for children. She also exhibited her paintings in solo and group exhibitions in many countries, receiving honors in Italy, Germany, Iran, Austria, India, France, Spain and Slovakia. Nasrin won the Grand Prize at the Noma Concours in Japan and was selected as best illustrator at the Tehran International Biennial of Illustrations for the paintings that now appear in this new version of the Thumbelina story. She was also nominated for the prestigious Hans Christian Andersen Award and the UNICEF Ezra Jack Keats International Award for Excellence in Children's Book Illustration. She spent her last years painting, and living with her family in Canada.